Text copyright © 2012 by Jorge Luján
Illustrations copyright © 2012 by Chiara Carrer
English translation copyright © 2012 by Elisa Amado
Published in Canada and the USA in 2012 by Groundwood Books

Groundwood Books / House of Anansi Press
110 Spadina Avenue, Suite 801, Toronto, Ontario M5V 2K4
or c/o Publishers Group West
1700 Fourth Street, Berkeley, CA 94710

We acknowledge for their financial support of our publishing program
the Government of Canada through the Canada Book Fund (CBF).

Library and Archives Canada Cataloguing in Publication

Luján, Jorge
Stephen and the beetle / Jorge Luján, author ; Chiara Carrer,
illustrator ; Elisa Amado, translator.

ISBN 978-1-55498-192-2

I. Carrer, Chiara II. Amado, Elisa III. Title.

PZ7.L987St 2012   j863'.7   C2012-900744-7

The illustrations were done in acrylic, ink, pencil, oil pastel and collage.
Design by Michael Solomon
Printed and bound in China

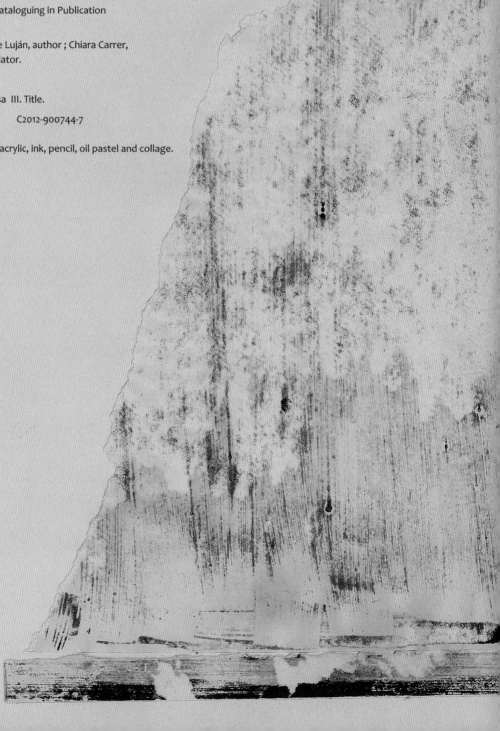

Stephen
and the
Beetle

Jorge Luján
Chiara Carrer

Translated by Elisa Amado

GROUNDWOOD BOOKS

HOUSE OF ANANSI PRESS

Toronto   Berkeley

One afternoon...

Stephen saw a beetle.

He took off his shoe
and raised his arm.

The beetle went on about its business. It had no idea what was about to happen.

Stephen lifted his shoe higher,
but suddenly a thought came
into his head.

Where was the beetle going, anyway?
To which corner of the garden?
And what for?

If I drop my shoe, thought Stephen,
the day will go on just the same,
except for one small thing.

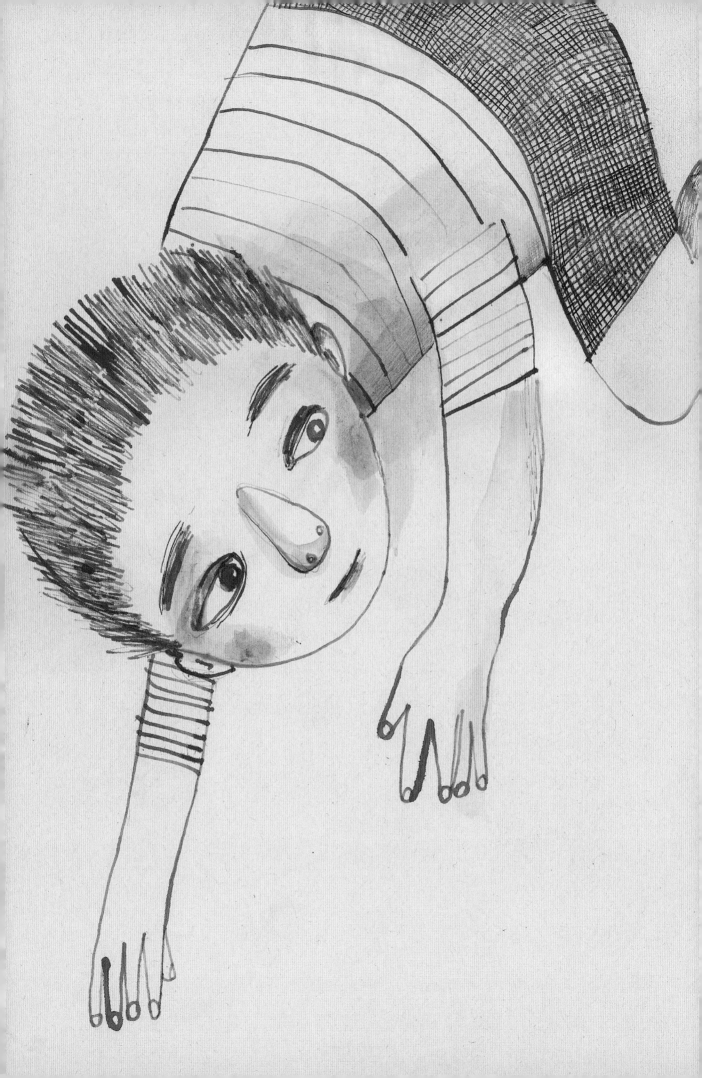

So he put down his shoe and, laying his
head on the ground...

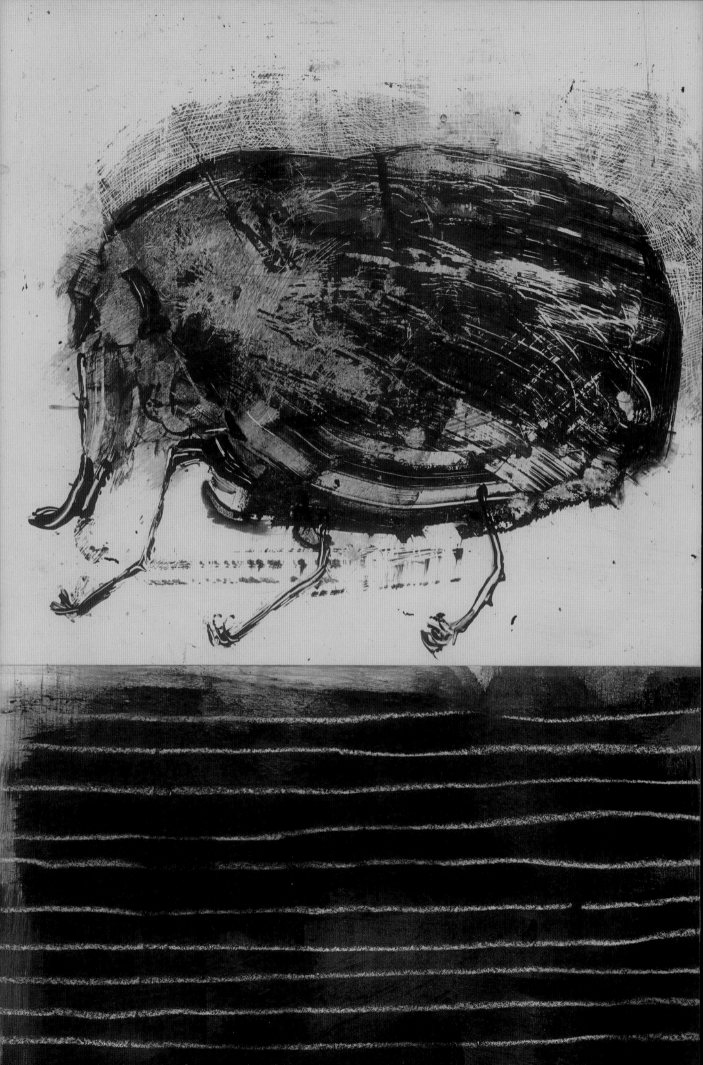

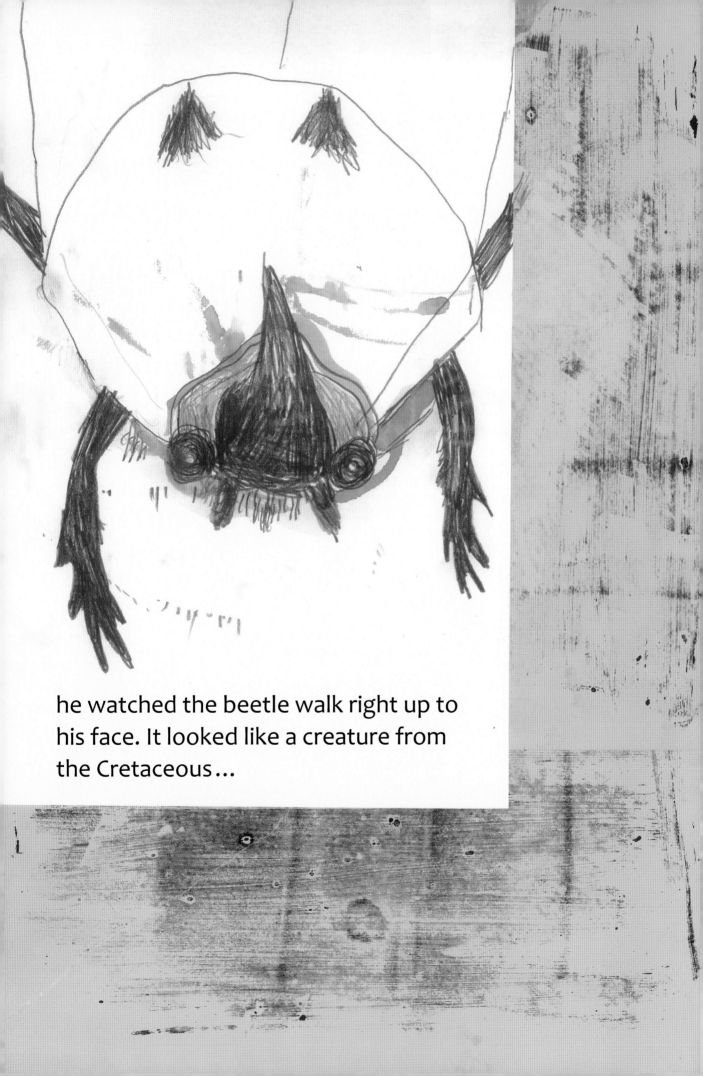

he watched the beetle walk right up to his face. It looked like a creature from the Cretaceous...

a terrible triceratops that lifted its glistening
horns, waved its huge hoofs in the air and,
just as it was about to attack…

seemed to remember something.
The beetle dropped down on all
four feet, turned aside…

and slowly walked off, making
its way to the furthest corner
of the garden.